My name is not

My name is

And this is my

TWO HOOTS *book*

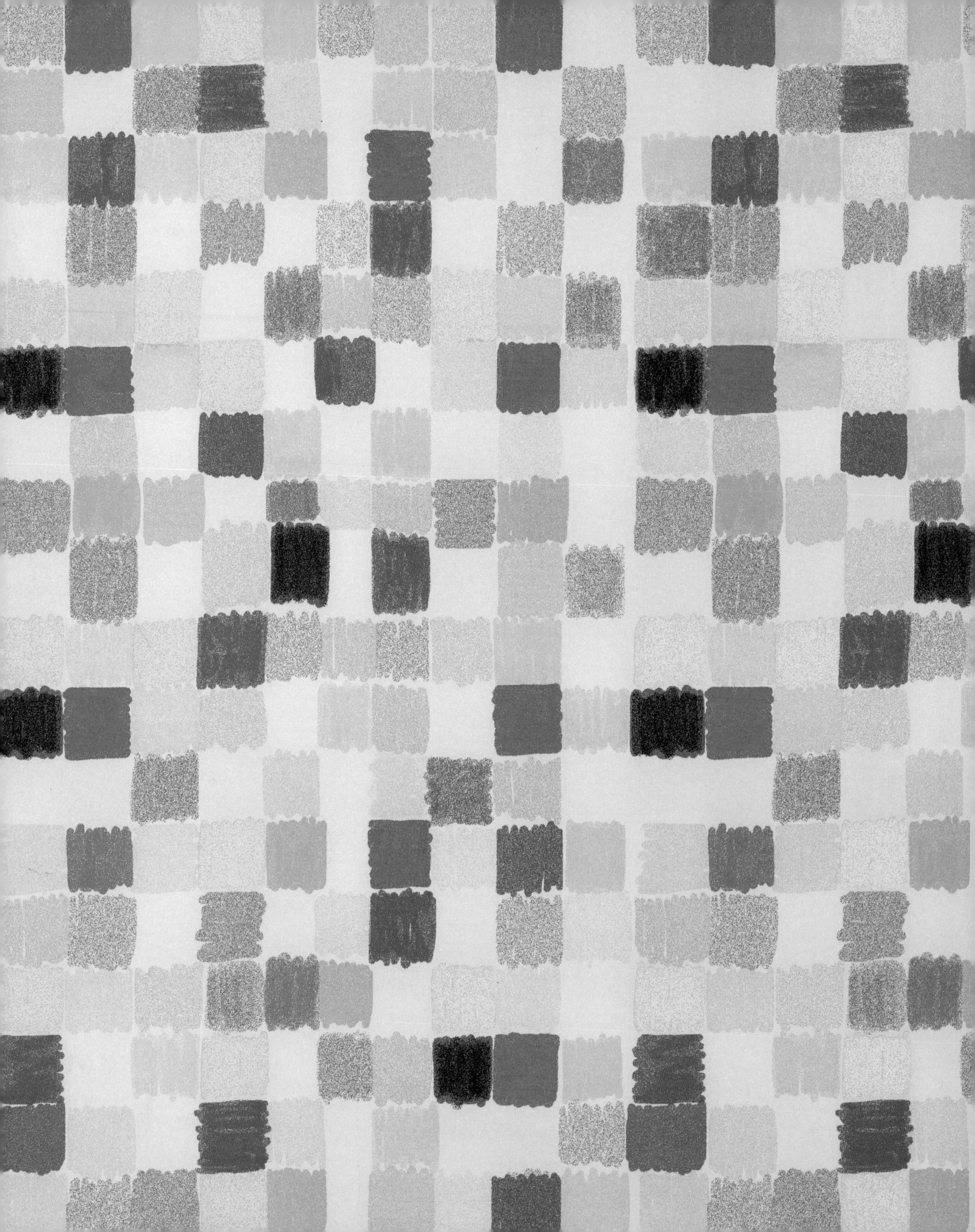

For Mum and Dad - B.M.

First published 2020 by Two Hoots
This edition published 2021 by Two Hoots
an imprint of Pan Macmillan
The Smithson
6 Briset Street
London
EC1M 5NR

Associated companies around the world
www.panmacmillan.com
ISBN: 978-1-5098-8225-0

1 3 5 7 9 8 6 4 2
A CIP catalogue record for this book is available from the British Library.
Printed in China
The illustrations in this book were created using Photoshop.

With thanks to Suzanne Carnell, Sharon King-Chai,
Jenny Shone, Kaltoun Yusuf, Tony Fleetwood and Helen Weir.

www.twohootsbooks.com

Ben Manley

Aurélie Guillerey

ALBERT TALBOT, MASTER OF DISGUISE

“Wake up, Albert!”

"Albert! Wake up."

My name is Clate Stouderhoofen, Notorious Desperado, and I cannot leave my hideout as I am a wanted man.

SALOON
SHERIFF

"Are you ready, Albert?"

My name
is not
Albert.

My name is Rusti Buffels, Fearless Mountaineer.
I am the man who climbed Mount Chirrachit,
and I was born ready.

THE INFERNAL STAIRCASE
THE SHATTERED GLACIER
SUMMIT OF MOUNT CHIRRACHIT
THE GRANITE GIANT

“What do you have for us today, Albert?”

TODAY:
ALBERT
My name is not Albert.

My name is Professor Octavius Pickleswick, Mechanical Engineer, and I am delighted to present to you my greatest invention.

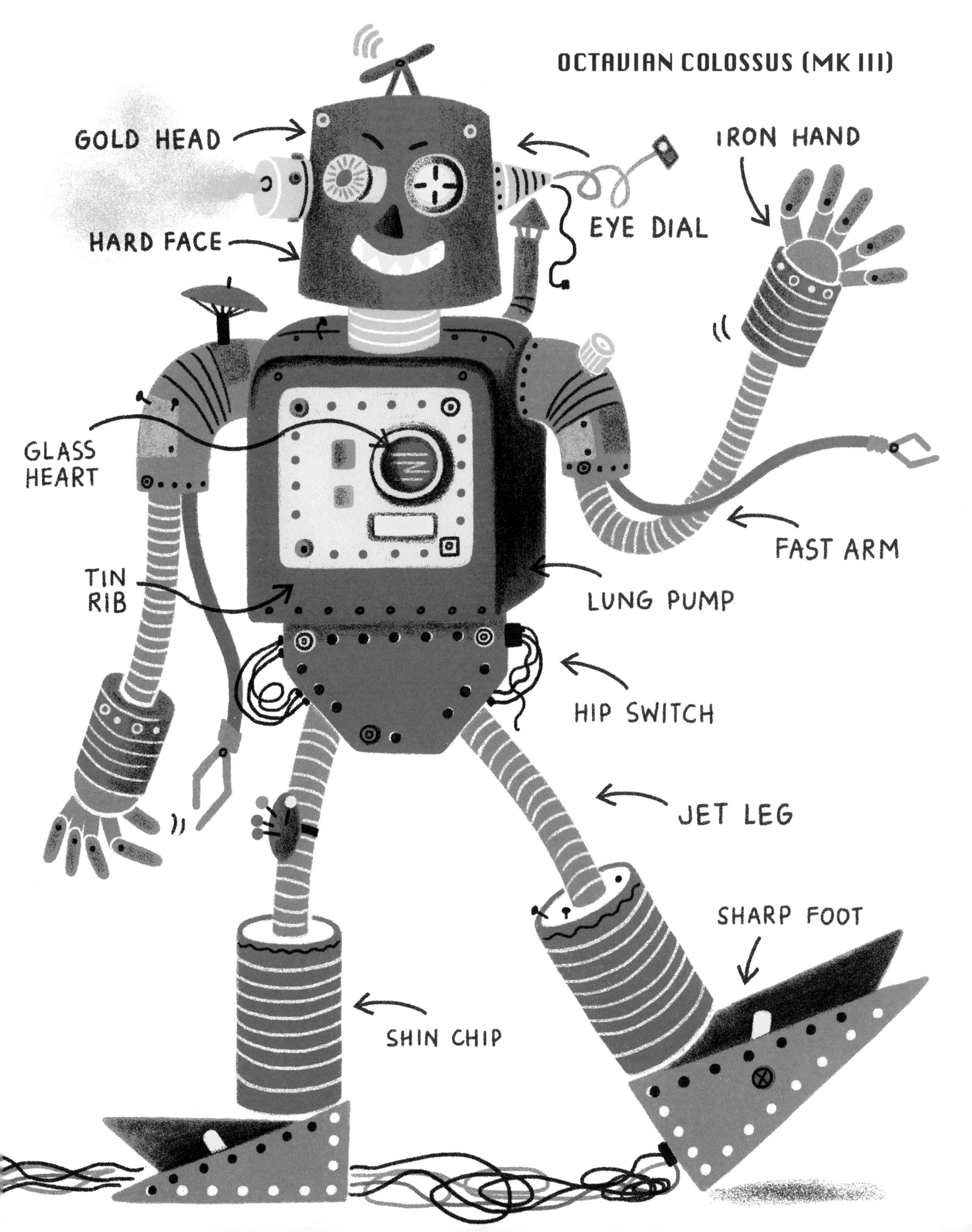
OCTAVIAN COLOSSUS (MK III)
GOLD HEAD
IRON HAND
EYE DIAL
HARD FACE
GLASS HEART
FAST ARM
TIN RIB
LUNG PUMP
HIP SWITCH
JET LEG
SHARP FOOT
SHIN CHIP

"Albert Talbot, jump in!"

My name is not Albert.

My name is Zandrian Delaclair, Antarctic Submariner, and I must keep my promise to destroy the abominable Vampire Cuttlefish.

URGENT
ARRIVE TUESDAY BY SEA PLANE.
WILL FIND THAT CUTTLEFISH AND THUMP IT.
OR NAME NOT ZANDRIAN DELACLAIR, ANTARCTIC SUBMARINER.
ZANDRIAN DELACLAIR, ANTARCTIC SUBMARINER

"Dinner time,
Albert!"

My name is not Albert.

My name is Anselom Facklejacket, Diamond Thief,
and I will take my dinner at the card table.

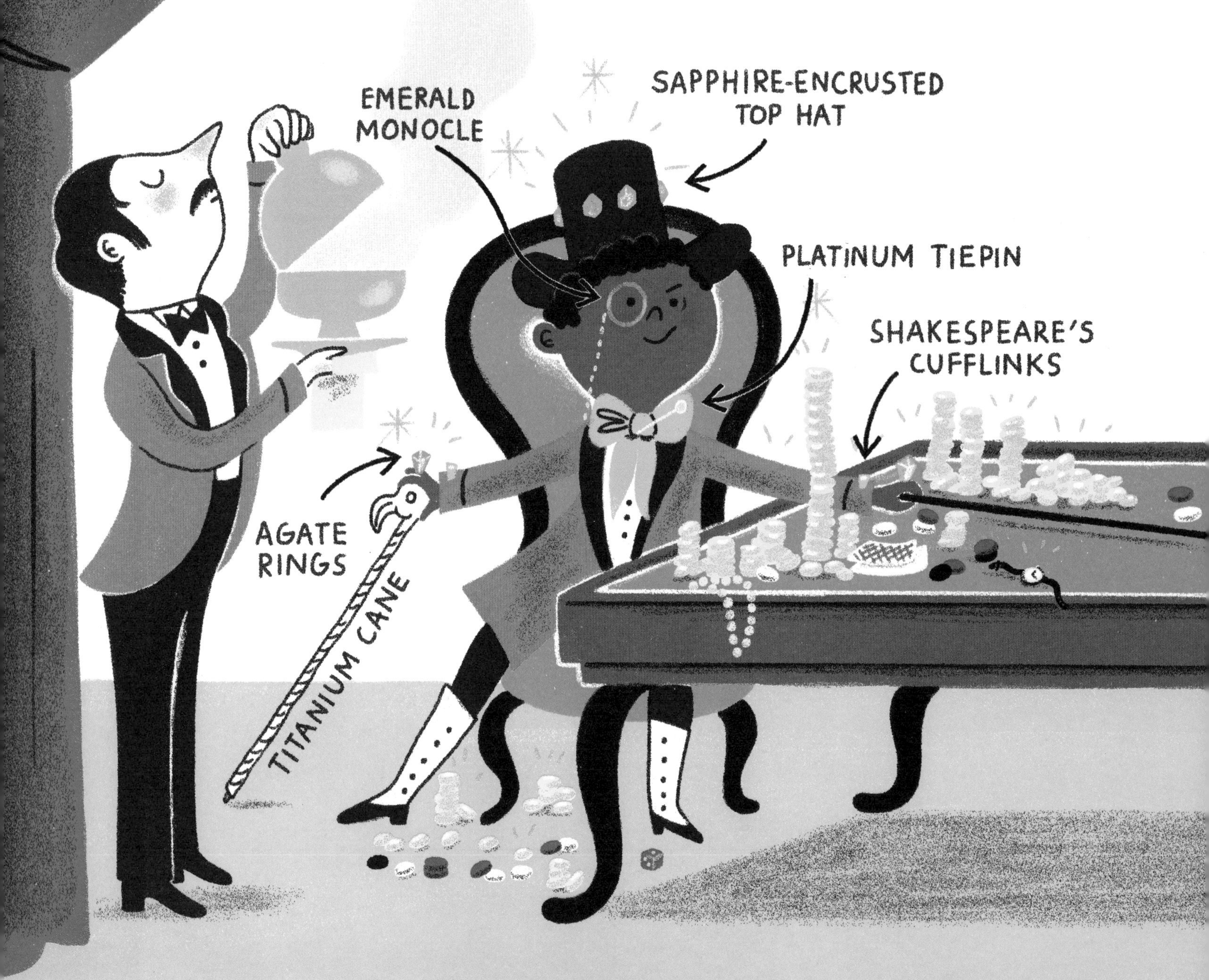

“Go to bed,
Albert.”
“My name
is not
Albert.”
FAR WEST

"My name is
Xarlon Quarkstar, Galactic
Megalord, and I won't go
to bed until I have taken
over the universe."

"Go to bed,
Xarlon."

"Goodnight, Xarlon."

"My name is not Xarlon.
I don't want to take over the universe
right now. I just want to be me.
My name is Albert."

"Goodnight, Albert."
"Goodnight."

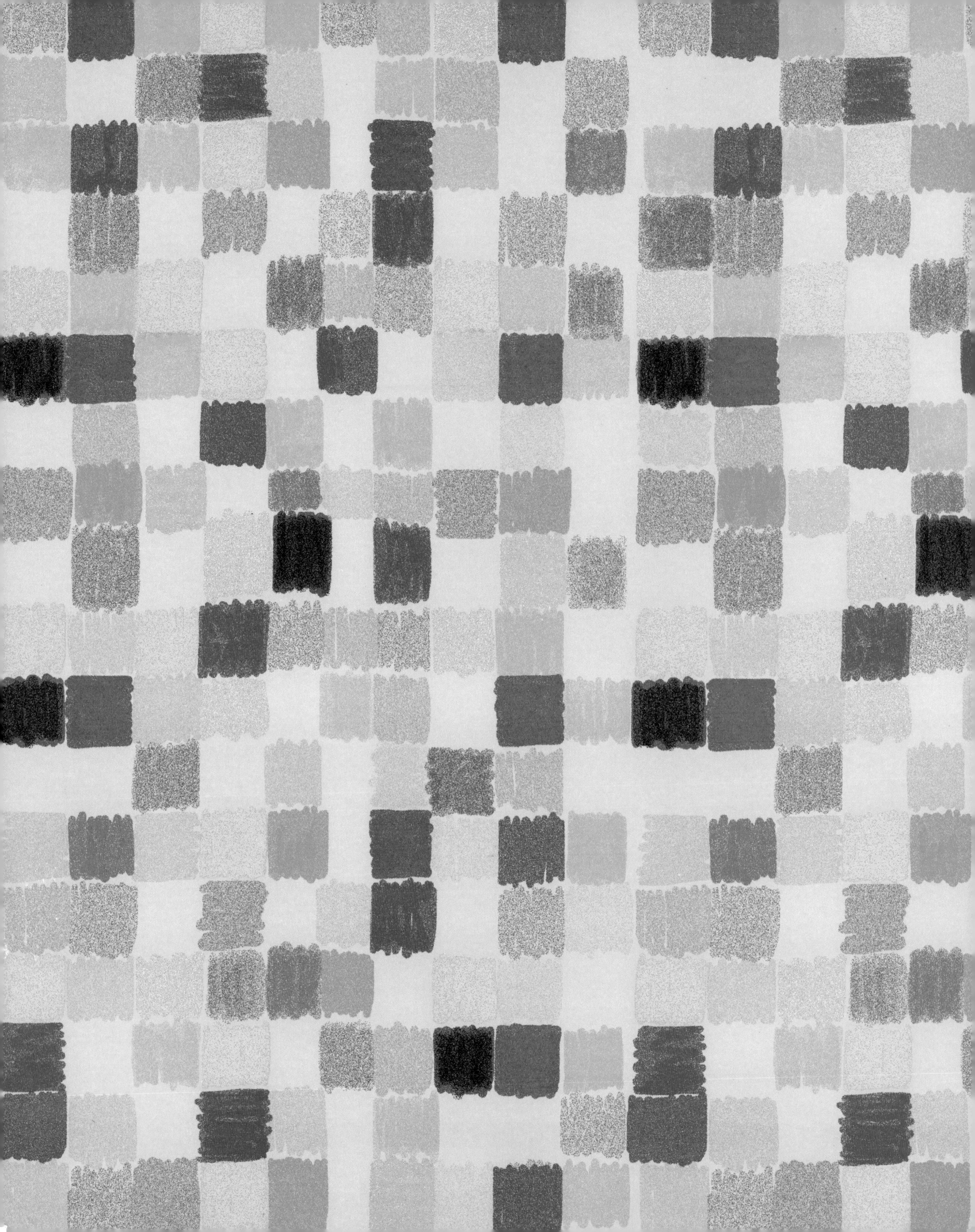

About the Illustrator

Aurélie Guillerey was born in the beautiful city of Besançon, France. She studied fine arts and decoration in Strasbourg. Since graduating she has illustrated many books. Her work is greatly influenced by the designers and illustrators of the 1950's and 1960's. Aurélie also loves fashion, and creating lively characters who live in busy environments. For this book she especially loved drawing Albert pretending to be an engineer and driving his gigantic robot, Octavian Colossus.

About the Author

My name is not Ben Manley. My name is Caraltan Naptrap, Supernatural Detective and I cannot write this biography right now as I am investigating unsolved crimes with just a little help from the ghost of Sherlock Holmes.